For Asha, Maya and Torah
(whose Mums are no trouble at all!)

Library of Congress Cataloging in Publication Data
Cole, Babette.
    The trouble with mom.
Summary: A young boy's mother, who is a witch, is
not immediately accepted by the parents of the children
in his new school.
[1. Witch—Fiction.   2. Mothers—Fiction]
I Title.
PZ7.C6734Tr   1984   [E]   83-7750
ISBN 0-698-20597-9
pbk ISBN 0-698-20624-X

The Trouble with Mom

Babette Cole

Coward-McCann, Inc., New York

The trouble with
mom is the hats
she wears. . .

At first the other kids gave me funny looks when

she took me to my new school. . .

She didn't seem to get along. . .

with the other parents.

They kept asking me where my dad was.
Mom says he's staying put until
he stops going bowling every night.

Teacher asked us if our moms would make cupcakes for the PTA meeting.

Mom made some.

They were a disaster,
but the kids thought they were
BRILLIANT!

They asked if they could come and play
at my house.

I didn't know
what they would
think of it!

Their parents said
they couldn't come,
but they came
anyway.

They liked our pets.

They met Granny.

Mom behaved very well.

We all went wild!

Then their parents turned up
and ruined everything.

They told Mom off.

Mom
was
sad.

My new friends were fed up.
They said, "Your mom's O.K. But we're
not allowed to come and play any more."

Then one day the school caught fire.
We thought we were going to roast.

Mom beat all the fire engines!

She put out the fire
before any of
the other parents
arrived.

They couldn't thank her enough.

Now we all go wild
at my house.